JACK
IN A BOX

by DIANE CAPRI

Published by: AugustBooks
http://www.AugustBooks.com

ISBN-13: 978-1-940768-28-1

Original cover design by jeroentenberge.com
Interior layout by Author E.M.S.

Published in the United States of America.

Visit the author website:
http://www.DianeCapri.com

ALSO BY DIANE CAPRI

JACK

IN A BOX

For Lee Child, with unrelenting gratitude.

CHAPTER ONE

FBI SPECIAL AGENT KIM Otto's slowly descending eyelids abraded like forty-grit sandpaper along her corneas and rested briefly before ascending in gouging retraction. How long had she been sitting here? The FBI headquarters building was quiet here in the basement. Activity was limited to higher floors where essential matters were handled.

"What are you missing?" she asked the empty room as if she expected the answer to be revealed, when she expected nothing of the sort. If she was going to find anything at all, she'd have found it long before now. But she couldn't give up, so she thought it through again.

She'd begun by searching for general

information. Finding none, she'd narrowed her search to the fingerprints. Fingerprints never changed, never disappeared, never failed to identify. Every law enforcement officer knew a fingerprint was worth a thousand eyewitness reports and often better even than DNA.

But, like DNA, fingerprints were only useful when compared to known identities. Law enforcement files around the globe were filled with unidentified prints and DNA. The first order of business was to find proof of positive identity. She'd thought that would be easy. Wrong.

Jack Reacher must have been fingerprinted by the Army, like every other soldier. Maybe a single set of prints made all those years ago could have been misplaced in the days before computers ruled the world. Or maybe accidentally destroyed somehow.

Kim thought not.

Relevant military files were integrated with FBI and other agency files now, she knew. But Reacher's army discharge was long before 9/11. Back in those days, government agencies didn't share information in the way they did now. Some old files involving military personnel instead of criminal defendants were not searchable in the various FBI databases Kim had the necessary security clearance to examine without raising the alarms she didn't want to trigger.

Her plan was to check the military files last because they were the oldest. Her accounting background led her to prioritize the most recent information first, or first in, last out.

Reacher wasn't an army grunt who'd been drafted, served a quick term, and mustered out. He'd spent thirteen years in service to his country, including his last stint with the military police. As an MP his reference fingerprints would have been routinely used to exclude his prints from those left by witnesses and suspects at crime scenes.

Kim should have found at least a few Reacher exemplars in the FBI databases. But she hadn't.

Nor had she really expected to find anything relevant, although she hadn't abandoned all hope. But her realistic plan was only to confirm her assumption that nothing concerning Jack Reacher existed in FBI files. After that, she and Gaspar could move on to conducting additional interviews with victims, witnesses, reporting parties, and informants. Always assuming they could find any of the above.

"Coffee. You need a caffeine jolt," Kim said aloud.

She stood, eyes closed to avoid the gouging, stretched like a cat, then a downward dog, working the kinks out of her stiff muscles. She heard nothing but her own breathing. She stretched her neck and shoulders again before making her way to the elevator in search of java, nectar of the gods.

Kim pressed the elevator button and completed another round of stretches while she waited. Lights above the door flashed up and down and up and down, stopping at floors high above. The basement was low priority, below stops where others were consumed by important activity, Kim concluded. The only coffee at this hour would be inside the busiest sectors of the building, places she didn't want to be seen. Yet... She sighed, shrugged, headed for the stairs.

When she exited on the ground floor her personal cell phone vibrated. She checked the caller ID before answering.

"Good morning, Dad. You're up early."

CHAPTER TWO

FBI SPECIAL AGENT CARLOS Gaspar had
planned to leave early even before the classified
envelope arrived containing nothing but a copy of
Major Jack (none) Reacher's formal headshot; on
the back, a time and place for a meeting.

Had Reacher planned the meet? Or was it
someone else who wanted Otto and Gaspar present?
Either way, the big question was why?

Nothing traceable about the envelope or its
contents. He chased down the delivery service but
got no further data. The headshot was easily
obtainable by any number of people. Hell, he'd
been supplied one just like it when he initially
received the Reacher file assignment.

The time and place for the meet was a bit out of

the ordinary, but not alarming. The National Gallery of Art, East Building, on Pennsylvania Avenue. Ten o'clock tonight. It would be dark but not deserted. The building was one of those modern designs full of angles and shadows suitable for clandestine activities. But not a bad neighborhood, unless you hated politicians, and the entire town was infested with those.

He'd tried to call Otto, but her plane was already in the air and flying straight into an early winter storm. She hated flying under the best conditions; she'd be too wired by the storm and her errand to make any sense, even if he'd reached her. They'd talk tonight. In D.C.

Fifty minutes before he planned to depart, his bag was packed and stowed in the Crown Vic's trunk. He'd dressed in his Banana Republic suit. Gaspar popped another Tylenol, rested on the chaise lounge, and watched his youngest daughter from behind mirrored sunglasses that reflected little of Miami's winter sunlight and none of its heat.

Today was Angela's fifth birthday, meaning five giggling girls had invaded his home overnight. That was one of his wife's rules. No sleepovers until age five, then five girls for her fifth birthday, six for the next, and so on. His eldest would be thirteen in a few months; the idea raised gooseflesh along his arms and not only because thirteen teenagers in his small house would be ear splitting.

Thirteen was a dangerous age. Rebellion. Independence. Sex. He clearly recalled himself and his buddies at thirteen. The prospect of launching his firstborn daughter into that realm terrified him, but he acted as if it didn't. He shrugged. No way to stop the clock. It is what it is.

Gaspar felt his eyelids slide closed and shoved them up again. Yes, he was tired, but that was nothing new. Exhaustion had been a constant companion since his injury. He rarely slept more than an hour before throbbing pain in his right side awakened him. He'd become a quick-nap expert to capture missing sleep, but he felt his senses dulled, his reaction times slowed. The healed scrape where a bullet had seared his abdomen burned like a rash, reminding him to stay alert. He was grateful to have the fearless Otto as his partner, a solid assignment, and damn lucky to be alive to see his daughters' birthdays.

Cacophonous noise drowned such thinking. Five girls cavorting in the backyard pool, squeals, shouts, splashes. Surely decibel level ordinances in Miami's residential neighborhoods were violated.

He'd tried asking them to quiet down, and they did, but joy erupted again louder than ever after maybe five subdued seconds. Was impulse control equal to age? Would the quiet seconds lengthen to six and then seven? Would it be five more years before he might enjoy ten seconds of silence at home from his youngest girl?

He'd survived many life-threatening situations, but fathering frightened him more than anything. Four daughters already and his wife pregnant with a boy. Job one was keeping his family safe.

Before his injury he never considered such things, never worried that he'd fail, never gnawed the consequences. Maria had handled the girls effortlessly and he'd swooped in to count noses and grab hugs before bedtime. Confidence had oozed from Gaspar's pores back then. Four kids hadn't seemed overwhelming. He hadn't felt boxed in so much as engulfed by creatures he loved more than anything.

Not anymore. Adding a fifth child at this point terrified him. A boy. Boys needed a solid role model, a strong father like his own had been, but Gaspar's body refused to perform as required and he could barely keep his head in the game.

How would Maria manage the girls and a new

baby while he worked the Reacher file, traveled all over the country, only coming home for brief stints, not knowing how long this assignment would go on, worried that the work would end too soon?

He shrugged again without realizing he'd moved this time. It was what it was.

As Otto said, only one choice. He'd do what he had to do.

Men work. Husbands work. Fathers work.

He had to work.

They needed the money.

Twenty years to go. Simple as that.

But he'd bought a big life insurance policy. Just in case.

CHAPTER THREE

FBI SPECIAL AGENT KIM Otto had made a quick dash to Wisconsin over the weekend because Grandma Louisa Otto was dying. Not shocking, given her age. Modern medicine had pulled her through heart arrhythmias, osteoporosis, micro-strokes, and cancer, twice. This time she'd had another heart attack.

Kim doubted Grandma Louisa would actually die. Ever. Pure German stubbornness had kept her alive more than 102 years. Kim figured she had inherited the stubborn gene from Louisa.

But if death was to happen, Kim didn't want to be there to see it. She was not comforted by bodies in coffins or funerals or memorial services and avoided them whenever possible. Closure? Humbug.

"God knows how much longer she'll last, Kim," her father said, probably noticing Kim's lack of enthusiasm for the trip.

"Is mom going?" Kim asked. Her stomach was already churning at no prospect of playing referee between Grandma Louisa and Sen Li. Kim reached into her pocket for an antacid and slipped it under her tongue.

"We've been there all week. We'll return Monday," Dad replied, subdued. "Just go to Frankenmuth, honey. Say goodbye while you still can. You'll be glad you did."

In what universe?

Still, her father rarely asked her for anything. Sen Li had drilled into her children from infancy— when there's only one choice, it's the right choice.

So she went.

Just in case.

Kim had flown out early, before she could chicken out. Adding two plane flights to her life was never her first choice, but too often it was her only option.

Miraculously, the plane didn't crash and she made it to Madison in one piece. Frankenmuth Otto Regional Hospital was a twenty-mile cab ride from the airport. She'd booked a two o'clock flight back to D.C. God willing, she'd arrive at Reagan National by five-thirty. Plenty of time to take care of the things she needed to do before she met Gaspar Sunday. Get in, get out. That was her plan.

This could work, she thought, right up until the cab dropped her at the hospital's front entrance, when her internal response became, again, *In what universe?*

Nothing ever worked according to plan where her family was concerned. Dad had said he and his five siblings were posting a constant bedside vigil for Grandma Louisa, who had been a widow for decades. Kim shouldn't have been surprised to see the line of Ottos, all blonde and oversized, that snaked down the block from the hospital's entrance.

Mid-November was bleakly cold in Frankenmuth, Wisconsin. Men, women, and kids alike wore jeans, boots, and sweatshirts under coats, hats, and gloves. Practical, comfortable clothes. The kind Kim favored when she wasn't dressed for work. After all, she was German and oversized herself on the inside.

Only Kim's father had strayed from the family farm in Wisconsin, and he had traveled to neighboring Michigan at figurative gunpoint because his parents had refused to welcome his pregnant Vietnamese wife.

These Ottos served their community as farmers, shopkeepers, teachers, nurses, military, and a few, like Kim, were cops of one kind or another. Otto cousins lined up today because they worked during the week and Sunday was reserved for church.

Kim paid the cab driver and nodded to her cousins as she walked back to take her place at the end of the line. Shivering began immediately. Her suit was too thin a barrier for the Wisconsin wind. She turned up the jacket collar, stuffed her hands into the pockets, and shifted her weight from one foot to the other, attempting to gin up some body heat. The strategy didn't work well. Soon, the snowy concrete had transferred its glacial cold upward through the soles of her shoes.

Eventually, Kim reached the interior waiting room that had been overtaken by the Otto clan. She was in no hurry to approach Louisa's sickbed. She left the line and stood in a corner near the heat vent.

She absorbed the warmth through her pores while the noxious citrus-scented air purifier attacked her sinuses, causing a sharp pain between her eyebrows at the bridge of her slender nose.

She was too cold to make conversation, but no

one spoke much at all, and certainly not to her. Which was just fine. She felt as much an overwhelmed fish out of water as she always had among her fair-haired, blue-eyed, giant-sized cousins. None of the right-sized Ottos were older than eight and their conversational abilities would probably be all about age-appropriate video games anyway. The Ottos rarely spoke to her under normal circumstances; no reason to change things now. Kim shrugged.

As a child she'd wondered what it would feel like to be welcomed into this big, warm family. A long time ago, she'd realized she would never know that feeling. Every family needed its flock of black sheep. She was a Michigan Otto, born on the wrong side of the blanket as far as the Wisconsin Ottos were concerned. Period. End of story. She shrugged again. It was what it was.

A low murmur from the group interrupted Kim's thoughts and drew her glance toward the doorway. Attired in a full dress blue Class A Army uniform complete with ribbons, hat in hand, another Otto had entered the waiting area. Only one Otto was currently serving in the Army at that level, and only one Otto would compel the immediate respect that settled palpably over the room.

Kim had seen him maybe three times in her life before today and never in uniform, but she recognized Captain Lothar Otto instantly.

Literally the fair-haired boy of the moment, he sported the unmistakable Otto family countenance, complete with caterpillar eyebrows and what Kim's father called a high, intelligent forehead, also known as a rapidly receding hairline. He'd grown up in Frankenmuth like all the normal Ottos, attended West Point, and then served the Army and fought in its wars. She'd heard he'd been wounded two years ago, but he looked fit enough today.

Ottos were not a demonstrative bunch by nature and Kim observed Lothar make the obligatory rounds seeming no more comfortable than she would have been. Men shook his hand or saluted respectfully; women nodded and smiled or saluted; children kept their distance and saluted.

Lothar's identification was positively confirmed when he passed close enough for Kim to read his nametag, but he merely nodded toward her without stopping or noticing whether she nodded in reply. She didn't mind; she was no better at small talk than the rest of her family. She did not salute.

When Kim had absorbed enough real warmth to

feel her toes again, she became aware of the lateness of the hour. She needed to do what she'd come for and get back to Madison for her flight back to DC.

Yet the neverending line of Ottos continued unabated toward Grandma Louisa's room. When she could stall no longer, Kim joined the cousin trail, feeling as if the guillotine waited at the end of the line. The piercing pain between her eyes made the prospect of losing her head almost welcome.

Kim shuffled along with the line advancing at warp speed of two feet a minute, closing the distance in an orderly fashion as each cousin slipped into the sick room alone and stayed precisely sixty seconds before emerging without flowing tears or evidence of sobbing via fists-full of damp, crumpled tissues. Lack of hysteria salved Kim's anxiety; the inexorable forward movement did not.

Grandma Louisa had never inspired open affection from anyone and Kim wondered how she coped when her stoic progeny remained composed. Did Grandma think no one cared? Or was she, herself uncaring? This mystery had plagued Kim most of her life. Was it she who felt nothing for Grandma first? Or, as a small child, had she absorbed the message that Grandma Louisa felt nothing for her and defended against apathy thereafter?

Kim sighed and raised her hand to knead tension from the back of her neck. Again, she was glad Sen Li was absent. Mom would have created a spectacle of some kind about the Otto family's cold nature, the way she always did, and Kim had no desire to cope with such scenes on top of everything else. At the moment, Kim couldn't recall the precise nature of their last battle. None of it mattered any more. The old lady was on her way out. Whatever the source of their problems, now was the time to set them aside and move on.

Hushed words hummed quietly among the cousins at volumes too low to comprehend, Kim realized. She was sure the conversations were about crops and kids and church and plans for Thanksgiving. Nothing she would feel comfortable discussing with these near strangers, even if they tried to include her, which they did not. Not that it mattered. She'd be gone soon, and so would Grandma Louisa.

Too quickly, the Otto in front of her entered Grandma's room. The door closed quietly behind him. Kim was next and she had no idea what she'd say. She had not seen Grandma Louisa for ten years and the last time they'd met ended badly, as had most of their encounters. Grandma Louisa could not forgive Sen Li for taking Albert away from the family. That grudge engulfed Albert's daughters because they resembled their mother. Kim had accepted years ago that she would never be tall and blonde and German on the outside; it wasn't enough for Grandma Louisa that Kim was as fierce as any Otto on the inside.

Swiftly, the door opened, the cousin came out, looked Kim in the eye and said, "You're up. Good luck."

Kim considered whether it was too late to run, but she stood as tall as a four-foot-eleven-and-a-half-inch, ninety-nine pound Asian-American woman could stand, squared her shoulders and marched past the threshold, checking for a quick escape route, but finding none. Someone pushed the door and it sucked solidly shut behind her.

Grandma Louisa's bed filled most of the room. An oxygen cannula rested in her nose but otherwise she'd changed not one iota since the last time Kim had seen her. She wore a pink brocade bed jacket, her gray hair was teased and lacquered as usual, and her hands were folded on her lap, the better to display her rings and manicured nails. She wore pearl and sapphire earrings and a double strand of pearls around her sizeable neck. Mauve lipstick emphasized her still-full lips. Blush rosied her cheeks. Stylish eyeglasses rested on her nose visually enlarging her blue eyes to bowl size.

Louisa Otto, matriarch of the Frankenmuth Ottos, held court as she always had, as if she were not just the head of one sizeable but important farming community, but Empress Augusta herself.

Whoever had closed the door gave Kim a little shove in the small of her back, prodding her closer to the bed.

"Kimmy," Louisa said, a moment before she reached out with a strong claw, restraining Kim by engulfing her hand inside a big fist, holding tight. Rough callouses on Louisa's palm scraped Kim's skin.

Perhaps Grandma Louisa was near death, but she seemed a lot more alive than Kim had been led to believe.

"You look great," Kim said, clearing her throat and covering surprise as she leaned over to kiss a papery cheek dotted with lipstick from previous kissers.

Grandma Louisa replied, "I really do, don't I?"

Kim had to laugh. What could she possibly say in reply?

Not that Grandma Louisa gave her a chance. Maybe Kim's mind had misplaced the facts of their last argument, but Louisa's had not. She launched again as if the dispute had concluded ten minutes ago, not ten years ago. "Kimmy, I want to see you married to a good German Lutheran before I die. A baby on the way. Maybe two."

"You'll need to live a good long while then, Grandma," Kim said, struggling to eliminate annoyance from her tone as the old feelings flooded back. They'd fought bitterly ten years ago because Grandma had arranged such a union for Kim and Kim had secretly married already, not to a German Lutheran but to a Vietnamese immigrant. Kim was divorced now, but she simply refused to have any part of the old tyrant's nosey meddling.

"I will if you will," Grandma Louisa said flatly, steely-eyed and uncompromising. She squeezed Kim's hand tighter before releasing her completely. "Now would be a good time to find good husband material before you leave Wisconsin. I've lined up a few prospects for you to see this afternoon back at my house."

Kim felt anger bubbling up from her now toasty

feet, rising to levels that would have the family comparing her to Sen Li, and not favorably. Kim clamped her jaws closed and replied, "Thanks. I'm on my way."

She didn't say on her way where.

Grandma Louisa beamed as if she'd settled the fortunes of the crown princess. "You'll be glad when you're settled, Kimmy. Like your cousins."

Damn that woman!

Kim said nothing. She glanced at the uncles standing on either side of their mother, but neither could muster the guts to meet her gaze. She nodded, pulled her hand away, turned and left the room, saving thirty seconds for the next cousin in line, who was also single and probably wouldn't thank her for the extra time.

No one seemed to notice when Kim continued walking, out of the waiting room, down the hallway, and left the hospital through the front exit where Otto cousins continued to throng the entrance.

She stood at the cabstand and fumed, muttering suitable rejoinders to the old bat under her breath and louder epithets in her head. She barely noticed the frigid outside air for the first five minutes while the heat of her rage kept adrenaline pumping.

Where are the damned taxis?

Too quickly, the cold bulldozed into her bones. She hunched inside her suit jacket, stomped her feet to knock the snow away from her soles and keep her circulation going. It was freezing out here. Even colder than Grandma Louisa, if that was possible.

Why in the name of God didn't you bring a coat and boots? Better yet, why didn't you just say no, Dad, I'm not going. Not now. Not ever. Forget it.

Ranting didn't heat the atmosphere even one degree.

Global warming, my ass.

Kim felt her corneas might frost. She squeezed her eyes shut and shivered a bit more attempting to raise her body temperature. She wasn't going back inside to wait, even if her feet froze to the sidewalk and her eyelids ice-glued themselves together.

She heard the growl of an engine and opened her eyes expecting to see a yellow cab. Instead, a black SUV had pulled up alongside, Captain Lothar Otto at the wheel. He lowered the passenger window and said, "I'm headed toward the airport. Can I drop you somewhere?"

Kim wasted no body heat demurring. She hopped up into the passenger seat and immediately put her frozen fingers near the blasting heat vent.

"Frontier?" she said.

"Nonstop, huh? You can't be afraid of flying." When she failed to reply, he said, "Jumping out of moving planes, now that's a lot harder." Still no response. He took a deep breath. "Okay then. Dane County, Frontier Airlines it is." Lothar attended to driving the heavy vehicle expertly down snow-covered streets through towns unprepared for the early winter storm.

After she'd warmed up enough to sit a normal distance from the fan's blasting heat, Lothar glanced toward her and asked, "Did she give you the business about getting married and having babies before she dies?"

Kim nodded. She didn't know this man. She had no intention of discussing her personal life with him, no matter how angry she was.

He grinned. "She does that to me every time I see her."

"Really? I thought it was only me she subjected to never-ending ridicule."

Lothar laughed, the kind of deep belly laugh that only emerged from genuine mirth, the contagious kind. "When did you get so special?"

Kim smiled, felt better, almost as if she'd found an Otto family ally for the first time in her life, knowing the feeling was supremely foolish. Relief lasted about twenty seconds before the SUV swerved on a black ice patch and she grabbed the armrest to avoid being slung across the seat. She snugged up her seatbelt several notches.

Traffic slogged along, slowing their progress. Several vehicles less suited to the conditions slipped on patches of invisible black ice. They'd dodged two fender-benders already. Snow plows and salt trucks clogged the roadway, but drivers willingly waited as they passed.

Lothar concentrated intently on driving, but he must have sensed her anxiety because he said, "Planes take off in these conditions all the time around here. They'll de-ice. Two or three times if they need to. You'll be fine."

Kim's stomach started doing backflips and the two antacids she held on her tongue weren't helping in the least. De-icing two or three times? Seriously? Didn't these people know how dangerous ice on airplanes was? Didn't they understand that de-icing two or three times made crashing more likely, not less? Was she completely surrounded by hostiles here?

When they reached the curbside drop off for Frontier Airlines, Lothar turned toward her and placed a hand on her arm. "Hang on a minute. I have something for you."

Kim knew she looked puzzled because that was how she felt. Lothar reached inside his jacket and pulled a photograph from his breast pocket. He handed it to her.

She bit her lip to suppress a gasp. Major Jack Reacher's official Army headshot. She flipped the photo over and on the back was a sticker sporting typewritten information: Tonight. 10:00 p.m. National Gallery of Art, East Building, front entrance.

"What is this?"

"Following orders."

"What do you mean?"

"I was ordered to deliver that to you."

"By whom?"

"The point is someone wants to see you. They knew I could deliver the message. You understand?"

"Spell it out for me," she said, but she knew. She wanted him to voice her concern aloud so she would know she wasn't crazy. Because it was crazy to think that someone would manipulate her father to manipulate her to come to Wisconsin to meet a reliable cousin to give her a meeting back in

Washington D.C. which is where she started from this morning and where she was returning in thirty-three minutes if she survived her flight.

Lothar asked a question instead. "You recognized the photo, didn't you? How are you involved with that guy? Is he the reason you were so incensed at Grandma Louisa's meddling in your personal life? You're not dating that guy?"

He seemed genuinely concerned about her, which worried her more than the message. No one in the extended Otto family had shown her the least bit of concern her entire life. Why start now?

She said, "Do *you* know him?"

"By reputation. Otherwise, before my time. Reacher was discharged in 1997. Something hinky about it, though. His situation was definitely not normal, Kim. Wherever that guy went, bodies piled up. And I'm not talking about normal battlefield casualties. Nobody is that unlucky."

"What do you mean?"

"I'm a Captain in the U.S. Army. Like you, Agent Otto, I follow orders and don't ask questions, or I pay the consequences. Before today, I never had a problem with that because the Army never ordered me to do anything this odd; something not right is going on here."

No shit, she thought. "Like what?"

He shrugged, giving up. "Friends come and go in life, but enemies pile up. Reacher made a lot of enemies. You be careful, little cuz, or you'll never reach Grandma Louisa's age with or without those Vietnamese longevity genes."

A vehicle behind the SUV laid on the horn, letting Lothar know it was long past time to move.

Kim slipped Reacher's photo into her jacket pocket, popped open the door, and slid out to the ground.

Before she closed herself outside in the cold, Lothar said, "You need anything, here's my card. I feel responsible for you now. Don't let them be calling me to your funeral."

CHAPTER FOUR

WASHINGTON, D.C. WAS FULL of shadowy men these days. Some were harmless. Some were crazy. Sometimes it was impossible to tell the difference. Always safer to avoid confrontation, just in case.

He stood motionless in a shadowed doorway, an intimidating giant, waiting. He carried his broad frame tall and straight. He wore indigo jeans and brown work boots on his feet. Both hands were stuffed into leather jacket pockets for warmth. Fair hair fell shaggy around his ears and collar, his only cap against winter's cold. Sunglasses covered his eyes and reflected the weak sunset like cat pupils. Without visible effort, he seemed infinitely patient, self-possessed, self-confident, alert and relaxed, harmless and dangerous.

Few pedestrians raised their heads from the biting November wind enough to notice him; those who did veered wide, walked along the curb, as far away as possible from the boxy doorway. Just in case.

When the burner cell phone vibrated he pulled it out of his pocket and held the speaker to his ear. The woman's voice reported just the facts, "Messages delivered; on their way."

He said nothing.

He dropped the phone to the concrete, smashed it casually with the heel of his heavy boot, picked up the largest pieces, scattered the smallest, and walked unhurried toward Pennsylvania Avenue, dropping the rest into random trash bins along his route.

CHAPTER FIVE

AGENT CARLOS GASPAR FLASHED his badge at the entrance to the Pentagon, provided appropriate identification and after his approved visitor status was confirmed, he was flagged through.

As he expected, the building was busy even though it was five o'clock on a Saturday afternoon. Gaspar had slept an hour on the plane; Tylenol, the strongest painkiller he allowed himself, never lasted longer. He'd stopped for coffee after he passed security.

No one knew him here, but both civilians and military personnel were busy with more pressing matters. He'd passed security so they ignored him, likely accepting that his clearance was high enough. Which it was.

He glanced at the digital clock on the wall. Two hours before he'd meet Otto in the coffee shop. Plenty of time.

The first step in any follow-up investigation was to review and analyze all the previous reports. Because Otto and Gaspar were tasked by one of the FBI's most powerful leaders and assigned a rush under-the-radar project, this step hadn't been completed.

He knew where he was going, what to look for, and what he should find there.

He also knew he wouldn't find it. The absence of what should be present would speak volumes.

Archived service records, defined as records for veterans sixty-two years or more post-separation, were stored and open to the public at the new National Personnel Records Center in St. Louis, Missouri. Nothing pertaining to Reacher would be archived there because he'd been discharged in March 1997.

All inactive personnel records for veterans with a discharge date less than sixty-two years ago remained the property of the Department of Defense and its individual branches. In Reacher's case, that meant the Army.

Gaspar was an active, practicing Catholic. He

believed in divine providence. At first, it felt like he was on the right investigative path and he might find what he sought, even without an official archive. A fire had destroyed service records at the prior St. Louis center in 1973, but Reacher was only thirteen then.

But then Gaspar ran into several official gaps that concealed Reacher's history more effectively than youth or fire.

The Army didn't begin retaining records electronically until 2002, five years after Reacher's separation. This meant his files weren't retained in electronic format by the Army or electronically shared with the NPRC.

Worse, the Army's policies on maintaining and releasing service records were changed in April, 1997 and several times thereafter. The rules filled more than fifty-five pages, regularly revised, of course.

All of which meant that Reacher's records were once and should remain hard copies, resting in files owned by the Army that could be and probably were buried so deep in bullshit that no one would ever find them.

Unless.

Unless Reacher did something to get himself

inscribed by bits and bytes into the electronic records after he left the army.

Which, Gaspar was betting, Reacher had done. Probably many times. For sure, at least once barely six months after the army let him go. If Gaspar could find that record, he'd have verified hard proof and Reacher's trail might begin to unravel.

Gaspar knew Reacher had been arrested in Margrave, Georgia, and his fingerprints were taken and sent to FBI headquarters. A report was returned to the Margrave Police Department. Margrave PD records were also destroyed in a fire, which Gaspar was as sure as he could possibly be was no coincidence.

Even so, the initial fingerprint request should exist in FBI files. Gaspar had checked. The request did not exist in FBI files. Which Gaspar was sure, but could not prove, was no coincidence, either.

This was where the government's redundancy and repetitive nature might be harnessed, Gaspar hoped. The Margrave PD request and FBI reply should also have been noted in Reacher's military file, as should any request and reply about Reacher at any time from the date of his discharge until this very moment and into the future. Anything 2002 should be electronically recorded for sure.

And anything before 1997 might also have been updated because of the later electronic entries.

It was this army record Gaspar sought now. Positive paper trail proof of the legally admissible kind that Jack Reacher had been present in Margrave in September 1997, six months after his Army discharge, that Reacher was *there*. Not a shadow. Not a ghost. Not a rumor. But a real person.

Tangible proof of Reacher's Margrave presence was important because it provided the immovable, rock hard foundation Gaspar needed to nail down. His training said it was required and his gut said it mattered and that was enough for him. He and Otto were assigned to build the Reacher file and by God, he'd do it right, and he wouldn't make his wife a widow or his five children orphans in the process if he could possibly help it.

First things first. The Margrave PD print request and the Army's reply.

Then they would take the next steps.

Whatever those steps were.

And if the print request and reply documents were missing from the army files?

Starting here and now, he would confirm one way or the other.

Gaspar was a practicing Catholic. He believed in divine intervention. But he was an FBI Special Agent who also believed in hard proof and his gut. So he knew. He knew before he opened the box marked Jack (none) Reacher and sifted through the paperwork.

Relevant records ended when Reacher separated from the army in March 1997.

After Gaspar confirmed it, he and Otto could move forward. But to where?

CHAPTER SIX

AN HOUR BEFORE THE scheduled meeting, Otto and Gaspar stepped out of the coffee shop located across the street from the J. Edgar Hoover building into the mild autumn weather. Full dark had fallen awhile back, but streetlights and headlights and floodlights eliminated all blackness. The trees were partially clothed in fall finery; grass remained green and a few flowers still bloomed. No breeze ruffled to cool the temperature.

After Wisconsin, Kim found the evening weather pleasantly warm. After Miami, Gaspar might have been a bit chilled. Both were energized by the anticipated confrontation. Maybe they were finally going to catch a break.

Saturday night on Pennsylvania Avenue NW

was subdued. Traffic moved at posted speeds or less. Couples and small groups populated the sidewalks, strolling with discrete distances between them. Nothing out of the ordinary to notice.

Gaspar stretched like a cat, asked, "Shall we walk?" and set off eastbound before she had a chance to respond.

Kim ran through the options. The Metro Stop at 7th Street was off the path, a cab wasn't worth the wait, she absolutely wasn't taking the bus, Gaspar wasn't limping, and walking always helped to organize her thoughts before a mission.

"Probably easiest, if you're up for it," Kim said, quickening her pace to reach him and keep up with his longer stride.

So they approached the National Gallery of Art's East Building the first time as any tourist might travel from FBI headquarters, hoofing less than a mile along Pennsylvania Avenue, turning right at 4th Street NW, and walking along the sidewalk opposite the East Building.

Kim had studied the building through quick online research during her return flight from Madison. Opened in 1978, it was designed by I.M. Pei, which no doubt accounted for its irregular shape and probably explained the National Honor

Award from the American Institute of Architects in 1981.

Inside, the building housed modern art, research centers, and offices. Outside, it was nestled among the trees, surrounded by a six-acre contemporary sculpture garden and green space on three sides.

Although it was connected underground to the more traditional West Building where the main Gallery entrance was located, the East Building also admitted the public through a massive glass-walled entrance facing 4th Street.

Before they turned onto 4th Street, they'd seen a line of cabs and limousines at the East Building's front entrance. Kim looked inside the East Building lobby as they walked past. The room seemed stuffed to capacity. Men in tuxedoes; women in long gowns and short skirts; waiters passing trays of canapés and bubbly; a string quartet playing in the front corner. None of the noise from the party seeped out to Kim's ears.

"Some sort of charity gala?" she asked, noticing the flags on a few of the limos. "Diplomats, maybe?"

At the 4th Street and Madison Drive corner, they crossed 4th Street, turned and returned along the sidewalk closest to the East Building this time.

The green space was lighted, but too dark to traverse without dogs and Tasers. They stayed on the sidewalk until they reached the opposite corner, which was technically 4th Street and Constitution.

Gaspar's gaze scanned everywhere. He said, "Three dark hoodies at three o'clock, south side, between the glass pyramids. Check it out next pass."

"Reacher?"

He wagged his head. "Too small."

"You saw the sculptures and all those narrow, open areas around the building?" she asked. What worried her were the number of deeply shadowed areas suitable for clandestine attacks. Quick death was easy to imagine and bodies could lie in those shadows for a good long time before anyone noticed.

Gaspar seemed to hear her concern. "Even if he planned this—"

"You think he didn't?"

He wagged his head. "Not Reacher's style, is it? Based on what we know? He'd come right at us if he wanted to take us out."

Kim's breath sucked in and stayed there a beat. "Why don't I find that reassuring?" she said lightly when she could speak again.

Gaspar laughed. "If he planned everything. Big if. But if he did, this is a test."

"Test of what?"

Gaspar shrugged. "Dunno. He wants to see what we'll do. Whether we'll come alone or bring an army. How long we'll wait. What we'll say. My kids call it a psych-out."

Kim said nothing, but she agreed, partly. If she'd expected to find Reacher here tonight in the shadows, she would have brought more firepower. But she thought Reacher had planned this encounter. What exactly was he up to?

CHAPTER SEVEN

ON THEIR SECOND PASS in front of the building, the limos had begun to collect their diplomats and depart. They'd pulled up in front, one at a time, orderly, their drivers knowing the drill. The glass doors opened, spilling music and party chatter into the quiet.

Kim saw the three hooded people Gaspar had spied, standing between two of the glass pyramids. They wore dark jeans, dark athletic shoes, stood with their hands in their pockets, fidgeting, but otherwise seemed to lack menace. Impossible to discern whether they were men or women. Aside from the weather being too warm for hoodies, Kim saw nothing alarming about them. Yet.

By the third pass most of the guests and all of

the limos had departed. The string quartet was breaking down their equipment inside. Cabs pulled up one at a time waiting for fares. The noise level had diminished.

Kim checked her Seiko. It was ten minutes past their scheduled meet. What were they looking for? Waiting for? She had no clue, and on this point she judged Gaspar clueless as well.

Was Reacher here? Watching? Kim had looked for him but had seen nothing resembling a giant paying attention to her.

On the fourth pass, Kim noticed a woman standing apart from the building in the shadow of the largest pyramid, facing the line of cabs at the front entrance, facing her and Gaspar, facing the three hoodies, although they were blocked from her view by the large glass pyramid that separated them.

CHAPTER EIGHT

THE WOMAN WORE AN ankle-length black cape and silver party shoes with a three-inch spike heel poked below the hemline. The cape's full hood covered her head and obscured her face. She was slightly built, medium height. Kim could discern nothing else about the woman's shape concealed by her cape.

Kim felt her gun resting securely within easy reach before she touched Gaspar's arm. He nodded. They moved together into the shadows toward the woman. Despite the hour's walking, his limp remained under control.

The woman said, "No closer. I can hear you from there."

They stopped. Kim calculated how quickly she

could close the distance. Slightly faster than their adversary, since she was encumbered by those spike heels.

"What do you want?" the woman asked.

"You know that already," Kim answered and then asked her own question. "Who are you?"

The woman smiled briefly, as if the response was expected according to some tit-for-tat plan. "Susan Duffy, DEA, Houston office. Why are you hunting Reacher?"

"We want information about him." Kim hesitated a couple of beats to see if the woman would fill the silence. She didn't. "Why do you care?"

Susan Duffy broke the rules; she didn't answer the question. "What kind of information?"

"Everything, including his underwear size and what kind of condoms he uses. Whatever we need to get him in the box," Gaspar said.

Susan Duffy, if that's who she was, laughed.

Kim was vaguely aware that the departing gala guests had diminished from a few hundred to a few dozen to a few couples, making the trek from the entrance to the waiting cabs only a pair at a time.

Gaspar asked, "What do you know about Reacher?"

Duffy had tired of the game, perhaps. She simply stated the message she'd come to deliver. "You're wasting your time looking in official files. You'll find plenty before March 1997, but it's all bullshit Reacher prepared himself. You won't find anything involving Reacher after that."

"Why not?"

Duffy's expression was unreadable. "Reacher has friends in high and low places."

"Friends who made his crimes disappear, you mean?"

Duffy's tone hardened. "Friends like me. Friends who notice you making pests of yourselves in our files and repeatedly finding nothing. You don't want that to happen again. Not everyone is as understanding as I am."

Gaspar asked, "How do you know every file has been scrubbed clean of every Jack Reacher reference?"

Duffy slid the big hood back revealing short blonde hair, small ears close to her head, and huge emerald earrings. She put a bit of friendly into her voice. "Keep looking if you have nothing better to do. Your file on Jack Reacher will remain thin. Your mission will fail. You'll never put Reacher in any kind of box. And you'll piss people off. But hey, if you want to throw your careers in the toilet, you'll get no problem from me."

Kim watched one of the last pair of partiers walking toward the curb while she allowed this information to soak in. Both the man and the woman were older, a bit unsteady on their feet. Tipsy maybe.

She didn't know how she felt about Duffy's attitude. Challenged? Should she try to prove Duffy wrong? Or relieved? Because she could now focus elsewhere?

She asked, "Do you know where Reacher is?"

After a moment, Duffy shook her head, "You won't find him if he doesn't want to be found."

Gaspar's impatience flared. "We'll find him. We found Osama Bin Laden and he was a hell of a lot more powerful than Jack Reacher."

Duffy smiled again, "Yeah, we found Bin Laden. After ten years of looking. Yeah, we got him. After SEAL Team Six made it happen." She paused for the briefest of moments. "But we didn't take him alive. If you've got ten years and a SEAL team, maybe you can manage to kill Reacher, but you won't take him alive unless he wants you to." She shrugged. "Sure. Why not?"

Kim took a deep breath. "So what do you suggest?"

"You could give up."

Gaspar chuckled. "You don't know Otto."

The energy in the air seemed to shift, as if Duffy had done what she'd come to do. She nodded slightly before lifting the hood to cover her shimmering blonde hair and returning her hands to her pockets. Her slight form almost merged with the darkness and became a single shadow.

"Suit yourself," her disembodied voice seemed to echo too loudly. She softened her tone. "But know this: you risk everything if you keep looking. *Everything.* And Reacher risks nothing while he waits. That doesn't sound like a winning equation to me. Does it to you?"

CHAPTER NINE

BEFORE KIM COULD ANSWER she heard a loud thump behind her. She turned to see the three hoodies emerge from the pyramids moving swiftly. They approached the older couple leaving the gala.

The hoodies' moves seemed choreographed, as if they'd practiced or maybe done this many times before. One shoved into the distinguished tuxedoed man knocking him off balance; he shouted "Hey!" before he regained his unsteady footing.

At the same time, the second hoodie stopped, raised his arm, and pointed a Glock squarely at the older woman's chest. The woman looked green, as if she might vomit, and began to shake.

The third hoodie shoved the tuxedoed man

backward and shouted, "You got something to say?"

The man tripped and fell on his left side. A loud crack followed by the man's animal-like screaming confirmed broken bones, at least.

Otto pulled her weapon and aimed it at the first hoodie's center mass, and shouted, "FBI!"

Simultaneously, Gaspar pivoted on his good left leg, rushed the gunman, and knocked him to the ground, sending his Glock skimming the sidewalk into the shadows toward Duffy. The gunman's temple slammed onto the concrete and bounced twice, leaving him splayed and motionless, his neck bent at an unnatural angle.

The older woman's horrified face lasted three seconds before she staggered, fainted, and fell face down onto the sidewalk, breaking her nose. Blood pooled and seeped into view from the center of her face.

The second hoodie froze in place, arms up, hands palm out in recognizable surrender. Security reinforcements approached running, guns drawn.

For the next moments, Otto held the two muggers at gunpoint while Gaspar attended to the woman.

Kim glanced briefly toward Duffy. For the first

time, she saw a man standing alone in the sculpture's shadow. He looked familiar, but it was too dark to be sure. He was dressed in jeans and a leather jacket and work boots. Both hands were stuffed into the pockets of his jacket. He wore no hat. Duffy, completely engulfed in the long, black cape, passed close to him. He dipped his head to catch words that Kim was too far away to hear, or to be heard if she'd shouted to them.

Duffy never stopped walking. She disappeared into the darkness of the sculpture garden. The big man looked straight toward Kim long enough to cause a frisson of recognition to run up her spine before he, too, disappeared.

CHAPTER TEN

SECURITY GUARDS ARRIVED ON the scene, called for backup, secured all three hoodies, and assumed control. Minutes later, flashing lights from first responder vehicles lined up along 4th Street like a holiday parade.

Once the muggers were in custody, the tuxedoed man and older woman placed in an ambulance bound for the nearest hospital, Gaspar slipped into the shadows searching for Susan Duffy. But he found only damp November air, as Kim had known he would.

Gaspar returned, dipped his head to ask quietly, making the effort to return them to normalcy. "Now what, Boss Dragon Lady?"

"Like Duffy suggested, Zorro, we'll start where Reacher left off."

Still staring at the empty space where Duffy had been, Gaspar asked, "Which would be where, Susie Wong?"

Agent Otto turned toward Pennsylvania Avenue, smiled and replied, "We're building a file, Chico, not reading one. Think about it. Only one choice. U.S. Army buddies before March 1997."

THE END

AUTHOR'S NOTE

Thank you for reading my books. You're the reason I write! If you liked my books, you can help keep my work going by posting your honest reviews of the book to help other readers decide whether it's worth their reading time. I hope you will. You can find a complete list of my books with links to the book pages for reviews and other information at DianeCapri.com.

Please sign up to be on our Diane Capri Crowd mailing list so we can let you know when new adventures are ready and make sure you don't miss exclusive opportunities for free books. We'll give you a free short story simply for subscribing to my Licensed to Thrill blog. You can sign up for either easily here: http://dianecapri.com/contact/

If you want to read the stories Behind the Book, you can find them on my website. http://www.DianeCapri.com

Readers know our books are heavily researched, edited, proofed and professionally formatted. If you find errors, please let us know and we'll fix them if we can. We're committed to presenting the best possible reading experience and we appreciate your help. http://www.DianeCapri.com/contact/

While you're there, send me your questions. I love to hear from you and I answer whenever I can. http://www.DianeCapri.com/contact/

That said, the criminal activities herein depicted are pure fiction, as are the characters. Any events or real places mentioned are used fictitiously. As we all know, truth is stranger than fiction. We thriller writers are required to create believable facts, right?

Thanks again for reading!

Want to find out how The Hunt for Jack Reacher began?

Read on for an excerpt of

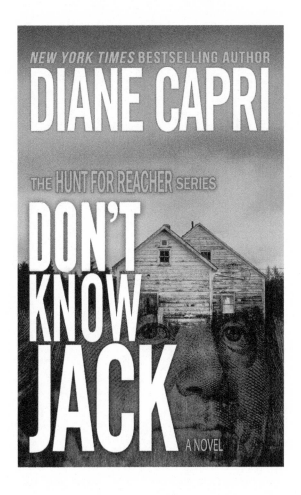

CHAPTER ONE

Monday, November 1
4:00 a.m.
Detroit, Michigan

JUST THE FACTS. AND not many of them, either.
Jack Reacher's file was too stale and too thin to be
credible. No human could be as invisible as Reacher
appeared to be, whether he was currently above the
ground or under it. Either the file had been
sanitized, or Reacher was the most off-the-grid
paranoid Kim Otto had ever heard of.

What had she missed?

At four in the morning the untraceable cell
phone had vibrated on her bedside table. She had
slept barely a hundred minutes. She cleared her

throat, grabbed the phone, flipped it open, swung her legs out of bed, and said, "FBI Special Agent Kim Otto."

The man said, "I'm sorry to call you so early, Otto."

She recognized the voice, even though she hadn't heard it for many years. He was still polite. Still undemanding. He didn't need to be demanding. His every request was always granted. No one thwarted him in any way for any reason. Ever.

She said, "I was awake." She was lying, and she knew he knew it, and she knew he didn't care. He was the boss. And she owed him.

She walked across the bedroom and flipped on the bathroom light. It was harsh. She grimaced at herself in the mirror and splashed cold water on her face. She felt like she'd tossed back a dozen tequila shots last night, and she was glad that she hadn't.

The voice asked, "Can you be at the airport for the 5:30 flight to Atlanta?"

"Of course." Kim answered automatically, and set her mind to making it happen.

Showered, dressed, and seated on a plane in ninety minutes? Easy. Her apartment stood ten blocks from the FBI's Detroit Field Office, where a helicopter waited, ever ready. She picked up her personal cell and began texting the duty pilot to meet her at the helipad in twenty. From the pad to the airport was a quick fifteen. She'd have time to spare.

But as if he could hear her clicking the silent keys, he said, "No helicopter. Keep this under the radar. Until we know what we're dealing with, that is."

The direct order surprised her. Too blunt. No wiggle room. Uncharacteristic. Coming from anyone lower down the food chain, the order might have been illegal, too.

"Of course," Kim said again. "I understand. Under the radar. No problem." She hit the delete button on the half-finished text. He hadn't said undercover.

The FBI operated in the glare of every possible spotlight. Keeping something under the radar added layers of complication. Under the radar meant no official recognition. No help, either. Off the books. She didn't have to hide, but she'd need to be careful what she revealed and to whom. Agents died during operations under the radar. Careers were killed there, too. So Otto heeded her internal warning system and placed herself on security alert, level red. She didn't ask to whom she'd report because she already knew. He wouldn't have called her directly if he intended her to report through normal channels. Instead, she turned her mind to solving the problem at hand.

How could she possibly make a commercial flight scheduled to depart—she glanced at the bedside clock—in eighty-nine minutes? There was no reliable subway or other public transportation in the Motor City. A car was the only option, through traffic and construction. Most days it took ninety minutes door to door, just to reach the airport.

She now had eighty-eight.

And she was still standing naked in her bathroom.

Only one solution. There was a filthy hot sheets motel three blocks away specializing in hourly racks for prostitutes and drug dealers. Her office handled surveillance of terrorists who stopped there after crossing the Canadian border from Windsor. Gunfire was a nightly occurrence. But a line of cabs always stood outside, engines running, because tips there were good. One of those cabs might get her to the flight on time. She shivered.

"Agent Otto?" His tone was calm. "Can you make it? Or do we need to hold the plane?"

She heard her mother's voice deep in her reptile brain: *When there's only one choice, it's the right choice.*

"I'll be out the door in ten minutes," she told him, staring down her anxiety in the mirror.

"Then I'll call you back in eleven."

She waited for dead air. When it came, she grabbed her toothbrush and stepped into shower water pumped directly out of the icy Detroit River. The cold spray warmed her frigid skin.

SEVEN MINUTES LATER—OUT of breath, heart pounding—she was belted into the back seat of a filthy taxi. The driver was an Arab. She told him she'd pay double if they reached the Delta terminal in under an hour.

"Yes, of course, miss," he replied, as if the request was standard for his enterprise, which it probably was.

She cracked the window. Petroleum-heavy air hit her face and entered her lungs and chased away the more noxious odors inside the cab. She patted her sweatsuit pocket to settle the cell phone more comfortably against her hip.

Twenty past four in the morning, Eastern

Daylight Time. Three hours before sunrise. The moon was not bright enough to lighten the blackness, but the street lamps helped. Outbound traffic crawled steadily. Night construction crews would be knocking off in forty minutes. No tie-ups, maybe. God willing.

Before the phone vibrated again three minutes later, she'd twisted her damp black hair into a low chignon, swiped her lashes with mascara and her lips with gloss, dabbed blush on her cheeks, and fastened a black leather watch-band onto her left wrist. She needed another few minutes to finish dressing. Instead, she pulled the cell from her pocket. While she remained inside the cab, she reasoned, he couldn't see she was wearing only a sweatsuit, clogs, and no underwear.

This time, she didn't identify herself when she answered and kept her responses brief. Taxi drivers could be exactly what they seemed, but Kim Otto didn't take unnecessary risks, especially on alert level red.

She took a moment to steady her breathing before she answered calmly, "Yes."

"Agent Otto?" he asked, to be sure, perhaps.

"Yes, sir."

"They'll hold the plane. No boarding pass

required. Flash your badge through security. A TSA officer named Kaminsky is expecting you."

"Yes, sir." She couldn't count the number of laws she'd be breaking. The paperwork alone required to justify boarding a flight in the manner he had just ordered would have buried her for days. Then she smiled. No paperwork this time. The idea lightened her mood. She could grow to like under the radar work.

He said, "You need to be at your destination on time. Not later than eleven thirty this morning. Can you make that happen?"

She thought of everything that could go wrong. The possibilities were endless. They both knew she couldn't avoid them all. Still, she answered, "Yes, sir, of course."

"You have your laptop?"

"Yes, sir, I do." She glanced at the case to confirm once more that she hadn't left it behind when she rushed out of her apartment.

"I've sent you an encrypted file. Scrambled signal. Download it now, before you reach monitored airport communication space."

"Yes, sir."

There was a short pause, and then he said, "Eleven thirty, remember. Don't be late."

She interpreted urgency in his repetition. She said, "Right, sir." She waited for dead air again before she closed the phone and returned it to her pocket. Then she lifted her Bureau computer from the floor and pressed the power switch. It booted up in fourteen seconds, which was one fewer than the government had spent a lot of money to guarantee.

The computer found the secure satellite, and she downloaded the encrypted file. She moved it to a folder misleadingly labeled *Non-work Miscellaneous* and closed the laptop. No time to read now. She noticed her foot tapping on the cab's sticky floor. She couldn't be late. No excuses.

Late for what?

The Hunt for Jack Reacher continues...
Read on for an excerpt of

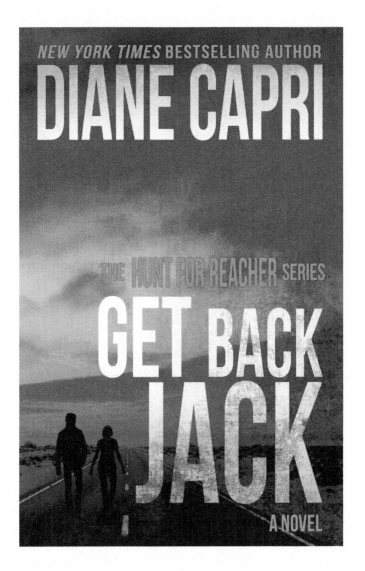

NEW YORK TIMES BESTSELLING AUTHOR

DIANE CAPRI

THE HUNT FOR REACHER SERIES

GET BACK JACK

A NOVEL

CHAPTER ONE

Friday, November 5
11:10 p.m.
Washington, D.C.

WHAT WOULD JACK REACHER do?

Sanchez considered the question again for a moment before he ignored orders and executed the scumbag with a single shot to the head.

At close range, any gun might have done the job. Sanchez had chosen a Glock 19, Gen 4. Utilitarian, tough, reliable. Comfortable grip, controllable recoil, easily concealed. Used by law enforcement because of its stopping power.

A perfect choice for a man anticipating precisely this situation.

Six and a half long seconds later, Sanchez punched the off button on the military grade speakerphone.

Connection terminated.

TWENTY-TWO FLOORS BELOW, the gunshot exploded through the eavesdropper's equally high-tech headset, traumatizing her eardrums almost as if *she'd* been standing in front of the bullet.

The crisp audio feed she'd appreciated for the past eighty-seven minutes and seventeen seconds was gone, as though she'd been dropped head first into a vat of clammy marshmallow cream.

Could Sanchez have gone off the rails at the very first obstacle?

She increased the audio to maximum volume and strained to hear his explanation, but heard only the severed connection's silence.

She jumped up, ripped off her headset with one latex-gloved hand and flung it to the floor of the four-by-four janitor's closet.

Christ!

She might have screamed.

Thoughts slammed like racquetballs inside her skull as she stormed back and forth in the hot, tiny closet. Even if she could've heard them, her sweat-soaked coveralls and paper boots no longer rustled crisply with each step as they had earlier in the evening. Behind her surgical mask, she sucked deep breaths and shouted silenced, frustrated curses.

She forced herself down into her guerilla training. Allowed fifteen more seconds to assess, analyze, plan, and perform.

Assess and analyze.

O'Donnell should have seen it coming. She felt slightly less stupid because O'Donnell had missed the obvious, too. Sanchez was far wilier (and certainly far crazier) than she'd believed. But O'Donnell had known Sanchez better than she did and O'Donnell was now dead. It was entirely possible that O'Donnell had committed suicide by allowing Sanchez to kill him now instead of torturing him later.

The two remaining targets could disclose what O'Donnell had refused to reveal.

Which meant her goal was still in play.

O'Donnell had made either a stupid blunder or a stupid choice, but his death didn't compromise her ultimate mission. She could still acquire what she'd come to collect. Her plan was altered, but not irrevocably thwarted.

Still, Sanchez's unsanctioned killing of O'Donnell was nothing short of disaster. For him. He had to know that, too. Which brought her back to the fact that Sanchez was far from okay. She must have missed something important about him. Something that might present a bigger problem. But what?

She hurried through her recall of the meeting she'd overheard. The erratic shuffling of Sanchez's shoes as he paced O'Donnell's office, pouring out his woes. At the time, she'd been impatient, stewing in her own sweat in the airless closet, willing Sanchez to get the hell on with it. She hadn't paid close attention to his ramblings. Mere impressions stuck in her memory. She ticked them off rapidly.

Sanchez increasingly distraught as he explained his plight, his anger growing while he recounted his five-year ordeal.

O'Donnell expressing shock. (Maybe he wasn't lying.)

Sanchez blaming O'Donnell, who claimed surprise. (Maybe he'd been a bit contrite.)

She cringed, recalling Sanchez's sudden switch from rage to whining pleas, begging O'Donnell to save him this time, as O'Donnell and the rest of their crew had failed to make the smallest effort to do five years before.

O'Donnell claimed he couldn't supply what Sanchez needed. (Almost certainly lying, of course, as thieves everywhere do.)

Sanchez's ordnance replied.

Then what?

Seven seconds before she'd recovered her wits enough to check the timer.

What happened next?

She'd been partially deafened by the blast. Her experience told her bullets blasted predictably into bony skulls, through gelatinous brain and out again, carrying moist soft facial tissue along with them. She could almost smell the gunshot, the metallic scent of blood.

Now, the office was no doubt a gooey mess, Sanchez was gone, and their perfect plan compromised. She'd failed. She'd need a plausible solution before she reported the damage, but that would come later, when she'd removed herself far enough away from the scene.

Now she was pacing again like an outraged tiger. She rubbed her face, and memory-pain sliced afresh; she jerked both palms away from the long-healed scars as if they'd been inflicted again by Sanchez's betrayal.

She sat on the janitor's stepstool, becalmed, ignoring the timer, backhanded the sweat from her brow and then stroked the narrow scar that stretched from the corner of her left upper lip to the outside corner of her left eye. Her index finger rested on the bump of keloid above her cheekbone, massaging absently, seeking comfort and clarity.

Rehearsals proved she could disappear in ninety-five seconds leaving no trace evidence. She should be outside the building in less than three minutes. But then what? Her escape plan was compromised because Sanchez couldn't be trusted.

Plan and perform.

Eliminate the hostages in Mexico. At least one. Immediately. Sanchez needed to know she was a woman of her word, to believe she'd kill the others if he stepped out of line again.

She'd intended to kill all of the hostages anyway. Right after Sanchez collected what he'd been sent to retrieve. His wife and brats would be of no use then. Sanchez's failure meant she was forced to revise—terminate one hostage a little early—and delay progress toward the goal, but only slightly.

Damn Sanchez. He was too smart to have failed so spectacularly. He'd no doubt planned everything.

What about her hostages? Had Sanchez planned a rescue? Changes were now required there as well.

Sanchez should never have betrayed her. She knew precisely how to deal with him. She challenged herself to remain still, kneading the pea-sized keloid like a prayer bead, while her mind raced methodically as if the devil himself snapped her ass.

Go now. Go now, her intuition prodded with each beat of her pounding heart inside the steamy, sweat-soaked cocoon that enveloped her.

Forty-two seconds after the gunshot, she was ready. She pulled off the wet protective gear, ripped the paper wall coverings down, stuffed it all along with the listening equipment into her oversized litigation bag.

A soaking wet woman fleeing a murder scene would be noticed and remembered in this neighborhood. She'd need fresh clothes immediately. She had none. She shrugged into her overcoat and turned up the collar. For now, she'd alter her planned route as she could and her overcoat must suffice.

She took one last look around the room, satisfied she'd sanitized as well as possible. She flipped off the lights, pressed the knob's center button to lock the door from the inside, and closed the janitor's closet solidly behind her. Sliding her gloved hand into her pocket, she slipped down the hall into the lobby and out into the Friday evening pedestrian traffic less than three minutes after Sanchez killed O'Donnell.

Six blocks away, cloaked by the late night crowd waiting for traffic to clear before entering a crosswalk, she heard her own voice murmur, "What the hell was that soldier thinking?"

Her chance to ask him came sooner than she'd expected.

CHAPTER TWO

Thursday, November 11
5:07 a.m.
Washington, D.C.

THE UNTRACEABLE CELL PHONE vibrated
itself almost to the hotel's bedside table edge before
FBI Special Agent Kim Otto awakened. She
watched the wretched thing snag against the table's
lip and let it dance an unrelenting jig for a few more
moments before she chose to answer.

Only one person could be calling and he
wouldn't give up.

Her assignment was off the books—not stated
to her as a mere preference, but hammered
home. He wouldn't have allowed anyone else to

use his secret phone inside or outside the Agency.

Kim slid her arm outside the cozy warmth of the down comforter, and brought the viper to her ear. "Don't you ever sleep?" she asked, not caring about the edge in her tone.

The Boss ignored her question and her foul mood. "How many times have you seen him in DC this week?"

"Why?" Not even bothering to ask whom he meant or how he knew she'd seen Reacher at all. She'd found staying under the radar a monstrous challenge in the era of constant surveillance, and had experienced the consequences of failure too many times already. She kept her conversations to a minimum; her face turned away from cameras, and used only the most secure connections possible. Even so, she was only too aware that more than one pair of eyes was watching her every move.

"Get in and get out today," the Boss said. "And watch yourself. He knows who you are and what you're doing now. He won't like you messing with his team."

Kim had already seen the results of things and people Reacher disliked. Not pretty. "Can't see that we have a choice, given what you've supplied us to work with."

Ten days ago, they'd been tasked with completing a background check on a subject being considered for a special assignment. Routine. Except the assignment was classified above her clearance and the subject was Jack Reacher and someone had worked very hard to ensure every paper trail ended with his discharge from the Army fifteen years ago.

For the first five days, she and her partner believed Reacher dead. For the next five, they'd learned so little about him that he might as well have been. Today, they planned to change their luck.

"You could tell me what you know," she said. "Or give us access to his existing files. Or do anything remotely helpful."

She listened to silent breathing for a moment, then tossed off the duvet and shivered with the cold shock. High-tech microfiber pajamas might be great for travel packs, but they certainly weren't warm. If she didn't get back to her Detroit apartment soon, shopping would be unavoidable.

"Check your mail," the Boss said at last, as if he'd only made up his mind to send her something during the call. "And be guided accordingly."

After that, she heard nothing at all. She threw

the cell phone across the room, where it hit the wall and bounced onto the carpet. With luck, maybe the damn thing would never ring again.

Sleep was now impossible.

Three hours later, showered and dressed and fully briefed on the short report the Boss had sent, Kim opened her door after the first knock. Room service. She signed for her meal, ushered the server out, and poured more strong black coffee. She snagged a piece of toast and spread a bit of jam over it. She wasn't really hungry, but bread would soak up the two mini-pots of coffee already in her stomach and reduce her antacid consumption. Maybe.

The next knock on her door marked the arrival of her new partner, Carlos Gaspar.

"Let's ignore the dead ones for the moment," she said as he walked in. "Any brilliant ideas about the others?"

Both had dressed for the same work day—hours of interviews in the business districts of DC and New York—but Gaspar's relaxed khaki was all casual Miami, and Kim's tailored black suit was pure, stodgy Detroit. They looked exactly like what they were, Kim thought. She found that refreshingly unusual.

"Look on the bright side," he joked. "Fewer interview subjects means less work. We'll make it home for Thanksgiving."

Kim's relationship with Gaspar mirrored the paradox of their assignment. Straightforward, but complicated. Easily stated, but impossible to predict. Reliable, but dangerous. In some ways, Kim felt she knew Gaspar well because of everything they'd already survived. In other ways, Gaspar remained nearly as much a mystery to her as Reacher himself.

Gaspar stood facing the window, watching the cold, grey November sky, preoccupied. His wife was very pregnant and alone in Miami with Gaspar's four daughters. Kim knew he wasn't happy about being away from Maria and the girls. And something very negative had happened yesterday in Gaspar's Cuban-American community while they were in Virginia following up a lead on Reacher. Something that worried him. Gaspar didn't tell her about the problem and made it clear he didn't want to discuss his personal business with her. She was glad. She had enough on her plate already.

"I'm waiting for that brilliance," she said.

Gaspar shrugged. "Brilliance? Such as?"

Kim watched him a moment. She was lead on this assignment and it was up to the leader to make sure all the players were fit for duty. Events had already proved the job was a challenge for Gaspar, given his injuries. Today's plan was routine pavement pounding and interviews.

Before the Boss's call, she'd thought she could afford to give him twenty-four hours to figure things out at home. After that, if the assignment continued, he needed his head (and as much of his body as he could muster) in the game. For now, she'd let that plan stand. But she'd do whatever she had to do, including replacing him, if it came to that. She wouldn't work with Gaspar if he couldn't do the job.

Like her mother insisted, when there's only one choice, it's the right choice.

With exaggerated patience, Kim recapped what Gaspar seemed to be ignoring. "Reacher's old unit had nine members, counting Reacher. We've spent two days trying to track them down. We were only able to locate three. We're set to meet the first two of those this afternoon. You were supposed to come up with a can't-miss approach for today's two. What are we going to say?"

Gaspar's tone was clipped, as if he were reciting

the phone book. "We're doing a routine background check on Jack Reacher for the FBI Special Personnel Task Force, updating his personnel file since he left the Army. We want to know, soup to nuts, what they can contribute to our almost non-existent data."

"Just like that?"

"Why not? The guy's a licensed P.I. and the woman's a forensic accountant. Both ex-Army police. They'll get it."

Kim drained the coffee cup and refilled. She felt taut as a drawn bowstring.

"He didn't call you?" she asked.

"Sure, he called," Gaspar told the view out the window. "He warned me about Reacher coming our way. He sent the report. I've read it. Nothing worth getting our panties in a wad over. Let's not get off course again just because he's yanking our chains, okay? We tried that last week and it nearly got us killed."

Now that they had at least an understandable plan, Kim wanted to stay on track, too. Despite running into dead ends everywhere they turned, they'd managed to uncover bits of Reacher's Army file that the Boss had refused to supply. They'd already tracked down two of Reacher's prior commanding officers. Both generals now, and both tight-lipped. Deliberately unhelpful, beyond suggesting they interview members of the elite special investigative unit Reacher had recruited and trained. For two years, the team had been inseparable, a force to be reckoned with, never messed with. If Reacher had kept in touch with anyone, the two generals said, it would be the eight other members of that unit.

Given what she knew about Reacher so far, Kim had her doubts. But a group of people once that tight could be a gold mine of information. Maybe. Besides, neither she nor Gaspar had identified any viable alternatives.

So, after unencrypting the Boss's early morning e-mail, they had even fewer.

She asked, "I wouldn't feel too optimistic about my life span if I were in Reacher's old unit, would you?"

Gaspar shrugged again, distracted, still gazing out the window—or at his reflection. "Special investigative units are manned by soldiers with a death wish, Sunshine," he said. "Volunteers for extremely hazardous duty. Natural risk-takers. Adrenaline junkies. They continue risking life and limb after discharge, too. Predictably, they don't live long."

She nodded. "True. But, Reacher's team never lost a member while they were handling the Army's extremely hazardous duty. They leave the service, and now four of the eight are dead, another is presumed dead, not one has died of natural causes, and their leader can't be found."

Gaspar shrugged. "The first one died in a car wreck. Car crashes kill plenty of Americans every year."

As if he'd said one member of Reacher's unit had died on a trip to Mars, she asked, "You believe that was an accident?"

At long last, he turned to her. "You don't, I suppose," he sighed.

"Let's say you're right. One car wreck. What about the others? Five years ago, one member of the unit disappeared and three more members died. All within days of each other. All three of the known dead tortured, their legs broken to immobilize them. And then each one dropped, still alive, from a helicopter miles above the desert floor. That is not normal risk-taking, adrenaline-junkie death-defiance, Chico. No way."

The data they'd uncovered on Reacher's army days had, as usual, revealed too little. He had never been popular with his peers. As a military policeman, Reacher was in trouble often and he'd made enemies.

But he'd been discharged fifteen long years ago and a lot of those enemies were dead or not interested in Reacher anymore. Unlikely Reacher would hide from anyone out to hurt him, anyway, based on the little Kim knew of the man. He was more of a confront-me-if-you-dare type.

So why was he living so far off the grid not even a sniffing bloodhound could find him? There had to be a reason, and the one she'd reluctantly reached was as good a working hypothesis as any.

Gaspar shrugged, wagged his head back and forth. "It bothers me that I'm starting to understand you. You're actually thinking Reacher killed four members of his own unit? Oh, and maybe five while we're at it, counting Jorge Sanchez, who hasn't been found yet." His tone conveyed precisely how preposterous he thought her suspicion was. "The Boss sure as hell didn't tell me that. Can you prove it?"

She said nothing.

"That's what I figured, Susie Wong." He grinned. "And what about the remaining three? It's inconvenient for your theory that psycho-killer Reacher didn't off them, too, isn't it?"

She replied, "We haven't actually laid eyes on them yet, have we?"

Kim wasn't joking. She'd believe they still walked the earth when she actually saw and spoke to them. All she could say for sure at this point was that she hadn't located death certificates for them. Where Reacher was concerned, the absence of records proved nothing.

Dave O'Donnell was first on today's interview list because he was located right in Washington DC. The other two, Karla Dixon and Frances Neagley, resided in New York and Chicago, respectively. Kim and Gaspar would be visiting Dixon as soon as they finished with O'Donnell, then back here tonight and head to Chicago for Neagley in the morning.

Gaspar turned from his window-gazing. "Don't worry so much. Mucking around with 15-year-old contacts will probably be another waste of time. But I get it. Interrogating the last three unit members is the only plan we've got. Let's just waste our time with O'Donnell and then we can move on wasting it with the last two. Have I mentioned lately how much I love this job?"

Kim didn't expect to get much help out of

O'Donnell or the others in tracking Reacher down, either, but she didn't have any other ideas. They'd finish the interviews in forty-eight hours or less. At that point, she'd demand that the Boss give her the resources they needed to accomplish the job or relieve her of the Reacher assignment. She had better things to do with her time and Gaspar was practically desperate to get back to Miami. This was bullshit.

She glanced at her Seiko. 9:43 a.m. They'd booked a 3:30 flight out of National to New York City to interview Dixon. That gave them plenty of time to interview O'Donnell and get to the airport. She grabbed her overcoat and headed toward the door. "Come on, Cheech. Let's get this show on the road."

"Yes, Ma'am, Boss Dragon Lady," Gaspar said. His tone was light, but Kim noticed his limp was more pronounced this morning, which too often meant he hadn't slept enough.

She was worried, even if Gaspar wasn't. She didn't for a moment believe the Boss had called this morning to warn her about provoking Reacher because he was concerned for their safety. Whatever the Boss was up to, her experience proved she'd need to keep her wits about her to deal with it. And she'd need a full-bodied partner, too.

She reached into her pocket for another antacid and held it in her mouth as the elevator dropped forty floors in twenty seconds.

ABOUT THE AUTHOR

Diane Capri is a *New York Times*, *USA Today*, and worldwide bestselling author.

She's a recovering lawyer and snowbird who divides her time between Florida and Michigan. An active member of Mystery Writers of America, Author's Guild, International Thriller Writers, Alliance of Independent Authors, and Sisters in Crime, she loves to hear from readers and is hard at work on her next novel.

Please connect with her online:

Website: http://www.DianeCapri.com
Twitter: http://twitter.com/@DianeCapri
Facebook: http://www.facebook.com/Diane.Capri1
http://www.facebook.com/DianeCapriBooks

If you would like to be kept up to date with infrequent email including release dates for Diane Capri books, free offers, gifts, and general information for members only, please sign up for our Diane Capri Crowd mailing list. We don't want to leave you out! Sign up here:

http://dianecapri.com/contact/

Made in the USA
Coppell, TX
18 April 2021

54025812R00059